Arty's Long Day

Arty's Long Day

By
Mark L. Redmond

Illustrated by
Laura Ury

Post Office Box 1099 • Murfreesboro, Tennessee 37133

Printed and Bound in the United States of America

CHAPTER ONE

All three stood there, gawking and grinning at us. I reckon I should have expected some teasing since Esther Travis was riding beside me. Never mind that Tom Green and Jasper Wilson were riding behind us.

"Ain't that Arty the Kid and his gang?" asked Bo Smith. He whipped off his dusty Stetson and held it close to his chest with both hands. He stood there, broad shouldered and well over six feet tall, and tried to look scared.

"I reckon it is," said the shorter, slim Chad Harte, our leather-tough top hand. "They can't be out on a raid, though." He elbowed Bill Munson, our bull-necked, bearded foreman who stood next to him. "Arty has a lady with him."

"Oh, I hear he always takes her along on his raids," said Bill.

"Now, why would he take that lady on his raids?" asked Bo.

"Two reasons," Bill replied. "First, he takes her along to protect the rest of the gang. That little lady is pretty, but she's also tough. Second, the gang rides a fair piece sometimes"—he winked at Esther but still didn't smile—"and I hear she's the only one who can find her way back home!"

Tom started to laugh first, then Bo slapped his Stetson against his leg and started laughing. Jasper, Esther, Bill and Chad joined them. I held on till I thought I was going to bust, then I had to laugh too. A few minutes later when we had stopped laughing, someone tapped my shoulder. Jasper had ridden his mule forward and stopped it beside Prince.

Leaning toward me in his saddle, he whispered so loud that even the hands couldn't help hearing him, "Arty, why was that funny?"

When I had stopped laughing a second time, I looked as sternly as I could at the three men leaning against the corral fence and said quietly, "Pack your bedrolls, boys; you're all fired!" I waved for my friends to follow me and bumped Prince with my heels. "Let's ride!"

"Just a minute, pardner," said Bill.

I pulled gently on Prince's reins and turned in the saddle.

"Mind if I ask where you folks are headed?" he asked.

"We're going for a ride," I said.

"I guessed that from seeing the horses," he replied. "Where are you headed?"

"South forty," I mumbled, turning Prince away from Bill.

"That's rough country," said Bill. "Are you sure—"

"I can handle it," I said over my shoulder. Now, I knew better than to interrupt a grown person, even when I was riled. I felt like I'd just stepped in a cow pie; I wanted to back up a step, but it was too late now.

"It wasn't you I was thinking about," he said quietly.

"I'm sorry," I said, turning Prince back toward Bill. "I just feel like a little kid when I have to tell you where I'm going and what I'm planning to do."

"He asks Bo and me and all the other hands the same question before we ride off for the day, pardner," said Chad. He walked over and patted Prince's neck. Then he looked me right in the eyes and said, "The Circle A covers a lot of territory, and there's no telling what could happen to even the best riders. If someone doesn't show up when he's supposed to, the rest of us had better know where to start looking."

"You're right," I said. "We want to do some exploring. I haven't seen much of the southern section of the ranch. That's why we thought we'd head for the southwest corner. We'll be careful, and we won't ride where the country is too rough. We plan to be back by sundown."

"I trust your judgment, pardner," Bill said. "Just remember the things we've taught you."

For the first five minutes of our ride, Jasper and Tom were the only ones talking. I rode, looking straight ahead. My ears were burning, and I had that same old knot in my stomach that I always got when I was upset. Being foolish in front of Jasper and Tom was embarrassing. Being foolish in front of

Esther was...well, I would rather have eaten a live tarantula. I could feel her looking at me. Sometimes I reckoned she could see right into my heart.

Esther and her family had been coming to the ranch for Sunday dinner about every other week. After dinner Ruth and Mary, Esther's younger sisters, would clear the table, then go outside to play. The grown folks would take a walk, sit on the front porch or go to the parlor, depending on the weather or just on what they wanted to do. Esther and I washed and dried the dishes and talked as good friends talk.

We spoke about what was on our minds—ranching, school, friends and other things. One of those other things usually wound up being my spiritual life. I hated talking about sin in my life, but I knew it was there. Esther knew it was there too. She most often brought up my being angry with God over losing Pa. She was never unkind or preachy, but she wasn't shy about speaking out. More than anyone else, she made me see that I had to accept Pa's death as God's will.

While she washed the dishes and talked, I dried them and listened. Esther had made me see that my being angry with God had stopped me from growing spiritually. It had also stopped God from hearing my prayers. I had been working hard at changing my attitude and accepting God's will. Now I had played the fool not only in front of Esther but also in front of Tom, who wasn't even a Christian.

"I'm proud of you, Arty," she whispered.

I grabbed the saddle horn to keep from falling off Prince. "Why?" I asked. "Because I did such a good job of making a fool of myself back there?" I still couldn't look at her.

"No," she answered, "because when you saw that you were wrong, you apologized and made things right. Everybody does wrong from time to time. How you handle your mistakes shows what you really are. I'm also proud of you because you used that silver tongue of yours to persuade Tom's parents to stop babying him and finally let him do something with the rest of us. Getting him to see his need for Jesus as his Saviour is nearly impossible if we only see him at school. There was a time when you were too bitter to be concerned about anyone else. You've changed since we first met, and I really am proud of you. Now, are we going to enjoy today?"

I looked at her and grinned. "Yes, ma'am!" I wanted to throw my hat in the air and holler, but instead, I just thanked God for giving me such a good friend.

The morning was perfect for a ride. Prince was feeling frisky; and if I had been riding alone, I would have let him run. Esther would have had no trouble keeping up. She was as good a rider as me—well, almost as good. I had saddled one of our gentle mares for Tom because he hadn't ridden much.

In fact, Tom hadn't been allowed to do anything much since he'd moved to White Rock. A year or so before his family had come west, Tom's older brother had been killed while climbing on some rock formation with his friends. I knew what the family had gone through, and I reckon I understood why they were so jumpy about letting Tom out of their sight.

From Tom's first day at school, I had felt that we were going to be pards. At school he had fit in just fine, and all of us liked him. A dozen or more times during the school year I had invited him to the ranch. He had been allowed to come once for supper—with his parents. They were not about to lose their other son.

When they had brought Tom to the ranch yesterday, they had insisted on seeing the horse Tom was going to ride. For a few minutes I was afraid they were going to take him back home. Esther was right. Although she, Jasper and I had been praying that Tom would get saved, we needed to talk to him too.

Anyway, back to why I couldn't let Prince take off across the prairie: Jasper's riding was getting better all of the time, but then I had seen him fall off a chair. I wasn't about to let him try a galloping mule unless there was a really good reason.

As we rode at an easy walk, Tom and Jasper moved up beside me on my left. When I looked at them, both were grinning.

"Thanks for inviting me to come along, Arty," said Tom. "Spending the night at your house with you and Jasper was a great idea. We got an earlier start this way and...well, I've never done anything like this before. Where are we going?"

"Nowhere special, I reckon," I answered. "I've

spent most of my time in Coyote Canyon or at my fishing hole to the north. I want to see what this corner of the ranch looks like."

"If you've never been where we're going," said Jasper, "how will we know when we get there?"

I looked at Esther. She was smiling.

"We'll probably ride until sometime around noon," she said, "then we'll find a nice place for a picnic, eat this delicious dinner Arty's grandmother packed and head for home." She pulled the brim of her hat down a little and looked at me. "Am I right?"

"Yep," I answered. "Since we have the whole day, we can stop to look at anything that's interesting. Keep your eyes open."

"For what?" asked Jasper.

"Anything you want to investigate," I said.

"Oh, we're looking for evidence again, aren't we?" Shielding his eyes with his hand, Jasper stood in his stirrups, stretched out his long neck and started looking around. "This looks like a good place for a—"

"No, Jasper!" I interrupted. "We're *not* looking for evidence. We found all the evidence I ever hope to find when we went to Coyote Canyon a while back. That's another reason I wanted to ride this way today."

"What about special men?" asked Jasper. "Tom and me brung empty cartridge boxes to put them in, and—"

"Tom and I *brought*," I said.

I shrugged my shoulders and smiled at Tom. Jasper rode beside me, looking at me and shaking his head.

"Well, now, Mr. Arty the Smarty," he said, "you interrupted me to tell me what you and Tom brought with you; but you can't remember what it was, can you?"

I looked first at Tom, then at Esther. Both were looking at the sagebrush in opposite directions, their bodies shaking with laughter. I gave up.

"What are 'special men'?" I asked.

Jasper looked surprised. "Don't you pay attention in school?" he asked. "Miss Ross asked us to get *special men* to look at when we go back to school. I got me a mess of them!"

Given a little time, I could usually figure out what Jasper was talking about. This time I had lost his trail.

Esther leaned toward me in her saddle and whispered, "Specimens."

"Oh, now I remember!" I said. "We want to watch for them for sure!" I wouldn't have traded a twenty-dollar gold piece for the satisfied smile on Jasper's face right then.

Esther and I laughed so hard and so often that morning that it's a wonder we didn't fall off our horses and break some bones.

CHAPTER TWO

Since this territory was new to me, I had no special place in mind for our picnic. If I had picked a place, we never would have gotten there. I reckon we didn't ride more than a hundred yards at a stretch without either Tom chasing after a specimen, or Jasper falling off his mount to chase "special men" he'd spotted somewhere close.

Now, Tom knew more about spiders, scorpions, grasshoppers, snakes and all kinds of other creeping critters than anybody else I'd ever met. He had books full of pictures, strange names for each crawler and all kinds of stuff I really didn't want to know. He had a bunch of dead things pinned to a couple of soft pine boards his ma had covered with a thick, gray cloth.

On a little piece of paper pinned to the cloth below each dead crawler, he had written its fancy Latin name. He kept those boards under his bed. He also kept some larger boxes under there with animal skeletons in them. It didn't seem to bother Tom, but I don't reckon I could have slept in that bed—or even in that room.

My point is this: Tom knew his business. The night before, I had handed him an extra pair of saddlebags and had watched him pack a little net and a bunch of small, empty boxes of different sizes and shapes.

Then there was Jasper. Jasper was the closest thing to a little brother I'd ever had. There wasn't a bit of meanness in that boy. I'd never seen him lose his temper, and he usually had a silly grin on his face. Still, without an ounce of ill will, Jasper could do more damage than an Old Testament plague. Now he was going to try to collect specimens. I couldn't wait to see what happened.

As we had ridden south from the ranch, the country had been the same rough, open ground I was used to. Boulders were scattered across flat land with sagebrush everywhere. We were early enough to see eight or nine small herds of deer. Coyotes slinking around in all directions were looking for mice, rabbits and just about anything else they could catch.

Tom and Jasper had moved ahead of Esther and me. They rode slowly, watching the ground. Suddenly they stopped, and Tom slid from his saddle. I reckon that Jasper was just too excited to remember what I thought I had taught him about mounting and dismounting. He should have gotten down on the left side of his mule, the side away from Tom. Instead, Jasper kicked free of the stirrups and slid off, feet first, on the right side.

Tom was crouching and reaching toward something we couldn't see when Jasper landed beside that big mule. It had never put up with Jasper's getting on and off the wrong side—that is, not without sharing its opinion. Its ears were back, and its mouth was open when it swung its head toward Jasper. I yelled a warning, and Jasper turned toward the mule. As he saw what was coming, he jumped back, screaming like a jaybird. The mule missed Jasper by less than an inch, but when Jasper jumped back to dodge that mule bite, he ran smack into Tom.

Now, maybe you won't think what happened next was funny, but I did. Tom was holding his little cloth net and was about to make a grab at something on the ground when Jasper backed into him. The force knocked Tom sprawling on his belly. Jasper sat on the middle of Tom's back with his eyes bulging almost out of his head and his mouth still wide open from his scream.

When Esther and I got to them, Tom was trying to get up. Jasper was still sitting on him with the same look on his face.

Taking Jasper's hand, Esther pulled him to his feet. I grabbed Tom under his arms and hauled him to his knees. He pointed to the ground in front of him and tried to say something, but his wind was gone. Something like a minute later he said, "Tarantula!"

Jasper pushed past me, threw himself on the ground and began to root around like a hog looking for a turnip. Snatching that little net by the handle, he turned it over.

"Is this a special—a specimen?" he asked, holding the net out for Tom to see.

"No, Jasper," Tom said. He took the net and

began to scrape something sticky from it with a twig. "This *was* a specimen."

No matter what the three of us said to him, Jasper saw everything smaller than a coyote as a possible specimen. We laughed till it hurt while he ran through the rocks and brush like a headless chicken. He chased jackrabbits, roadrunners, kangaroo rats, a prairie dog and even a young javelina. I almost choked to death on a mouthful of water from my canteen when he somehow threw his lasso into the brush and snagged an armadillo around the middle. He wasn't about to let it go, until we explained that we had no way to carry it back with us.

During the first three hours, Tom and Jasper did catch some critters. They had two big tarantulas, three horned toads, a centipede and four small snakes—all harmless.

By then the country had begun to change. We had ridden into some hills, climbing some gentle slopes and crossing a ridge. I knew when I saw the armadillo that we were riding into what Grubby called the "hill country." That was where the armadillo was easiest to find. That was also where the cougar was easiest to find. I thought of Phantom and shuddered.

"What's wrong?" asked Esther. "You have a strange look on your face."

"How can you tell?" asked Tom. "He always looks like that."

"I'm just getting hungry," I said without looking

at Esther. "Let's swing west around these hills and find a place to have our picnic."

Sometimes God says "yes" when we ask Him for something good. At other times He just gives us something good because He's our Father and loves us. This was one of those *other times*.

As we rode around the end of that ridge and saw the little valley there, nobody said a word. I didn't even try. The sight of it just took my breath away.

About a hundred yards away was a row of four giant cottonwood trees. They had to be growing on the banks of a creek—probably one that ran into the Guadalupe River. Close to the middle of the

level bottom of the valley were two small cotton-woods about five yards apart. The rest of the bottom was a deep blue, flecked with white like a horse's hide at the end of a hard race.

For a long spell all we could hear was a kind of sigh the wind was making in the trees. Then near the creek, a bird called, and somewhere close a bee was buzzing.

"It's beautiful," Esther whispered.

"Thank you," said Jasper. "Can we eat now?"

"Do you think," Esther said, smiling at me, "that Jasper is too big to be a specimen?"

"Not if we have a proper mounting board," said Tom, rubbing his hands together and smiling at Jasper. "Hold him for me!"

CHAPTER THREE

We dismounted and led our mounts across the meadow. Feeling the thick, green grass under my boots, I knew we were trampling the flowers; but they were so thick, we couldn't help walking on them.

"What are they?" Tom asked, stooping to pick a stem and sniffing them.

"Let me see them," I said, holding out my hand. I held them at arm's length and studied them. Then, closing my eyes, I pulled them toward me until they touched my nose. I took a deep breath through my nose, then touched the tip of my tongue to one of the blooms. Opening my eyes, I handed them back to Tom. "I reckon I was right," I said, nodding my head.

"Well?" Tom asked.

"They're flowers," I answered.

"Well," Tom said, dropping the mare's reins, "at least when we get back you'll be able to tell Doc O'Leary what you need him to pull out of your nose." Then he came after me.

Something like half an hour later, Tom, Jasper and I were laughing and panting while we tucked in our shirts and brushed grass and bits of flowers from our clothes and hair. We helped Esther, who was still neat and clean, spread a blanket in the shade of one of those cottonwoods. While she was laying out our vittles, we pushed through the brush and washed in the creek. By the time we got back to the blanket, our noon meal was ready. So were we.

While we were chasing each other all over that meadow, Esther had gathered some dry brush and built a small fire. From my saddlebags she had fetched a small coffeepot and made some coffee. As we sat down on the edges of the blanket, she was boiling water in a large tin cup.

"What's the water for?" Tom asked.

"I don't care for coffee," answered Esther. "I brought some tea."

"Do you have enough for two? I'm not much on coffee myself."

"I have plenty. It should be ready soon. Now, which one of you fine cowboys is going to pray?"

I was sitting across the blanket from Esther with Tom on my right and Jasper on my left. She let on like she was asking all three of us, but she was looking right at me. Then I noticed that while Jasper and I had taken off our hats and bowed our heads, Tom was already taking the second bite from a thick slice of bread. Paying no mind to anything but the tin plate in front of me, I prayed:

Father, we're much obliged to You for giving us such a pretty day, such good friends and such good food. Thanks for keeping us safe and for bringing us to such a pretty place.

Please help us to enjoy the rest of the day, and please take us home safely. Amen.

"Amen," Jasper and Esther whispered.

When I opened my eyes, Tom, red-faced, was putting on his hat. From things he'd said at school, I reckoned he and his folks weren't much on praying about anything, including their food. I don't know how things had been before his brother had died, but I knew that his family hadn't been on any kind of speaking terms with God since.

As much as I wanted to see that situation change, I also reckoned that my embarrassing him wouldn't help any more than my preaching at him would. Changing the subject seemed like the best idea. A chance to talk to him would surely come during the afternoon.

"Tom," I said, "you aren't used to my grandma's cooking. Since you're my pardner, I'm bound to warn you about that johnnycake. You just keep chawing on that sourdough bread and forget the johnnycake. In fact, I reckon you shouldn't even smell it."

"Why not?" Tom asked. He watched Jasper spread sorghum on a big slab of the yellow bread, then take a bite.

"Too dangerous," I said, shaking my head. Jasper was chewing with his eyes closed and a silly grin on his face.

"Jasper's eating some," Tom said. He licked his lips. "He's not in danger, is he?"

"He's been broken in slowly. It's like wading into a cold-water creek instead of jumping right in from a raft. You don't want to end up like that drummer back in Kentucky." I looked at Esther, and she rolled her eyes.

Tom had stopped eating. As he listened to me, he kept watching Jasper eat that johnnycake. Without looking at me, he asked, "A drummer?"

"A tinker, a seller of goods," I explained. "When he was passing through their territory, Grandma and Grandpa invited him to spend the night." I picked up a slab of johnnycake and took a bite. It really was good, and I could see Tom had a hankering for a piece.

"What happened to him?" he asked.

I swallowed a mouthful and took a drink of coffee. "Well, they meant to warn him about that johnnycake, but they never got the chance. Grandma must have gotten careless and set the pan too close to him. While Grandpa was giving thanks, he and Grandma closed their eyes. That drummer leaned over that johnnycake and took a big whiff of it." I took another bite and began to chew slowly.

"Arty!" Tom was almost doubled over from leaning toward me. Jasper had stopped eating and had laid down his johnnycake.

I took another sip of coffee. "Well, Grandpa was praying, but Grandma must have heard a noise or something. She opened one eye and saw the drummer fall over. When he smelled that johnnycake without being prepared, it smelled so good—could I please have some more coffee, Esther."

"Do you *want* us to hurt you, Arty?" she asked.

"It smelled so good," I said, "that the drummer's tongue snaked out of his mouth, slapped him up side the head and knocked him out cold!"

Tom's face never changed, but he sat up straight. "That's the dumbest story I've ever heard," he said. "Now, give me some of that johnnycake before someone knocks *you* out cold."

I tried to look hurt. "I'm only telling you what Grandpa told me," I said. "Have some johnnycake, but don't come crying to me when you wake up with a headache."

For the next half hour or so, we ate salt pork, boiled eggs, cheese and dried-apple pie. Then we stretched out or sat cross-legged on the ground and talked and laughed and sang. After a while I noticed that Esther was looking past me at something over my head. The wrinkles in her forehead told me that she was worried. When I rolled over and saw what she was looking at, I started to worry too.

CHAPTER FOUR

While I had been lying on my back, all I could see was a lot of blue sky and a few fluffy, white clouds; facing Esther, the view was the same. I reckon I had been paying more attention to Esther than to the sky, so I hadn't noticed that the sky behind me was a mixture of gray and black. As I watched, the blackness spread, moving toward us like spilled molasses spreading across a floor.

I had smiled the night before when Grandpa and Grandma had brought me the three bedrolls. "I know you always travel with yours," Grandpa had said, "but we wanted your friends to be ready too—just in case."

I had almost left the bedrolls in the stable. Now I thanked God that I hadn't. Grandma had wrapped each bedroll in a slicker, a long, yellow raincoat; and we were going to need those slickers pretty soon.

We packed up our picnic things in a hurry. As I worked, I was angry—angry with myself for letting down my guard. I had been taught to keep an eye on what was happening around me at all times. If Chad, Bo, Bill or any of the other ranch hands had been with us, they would have been watching behind me. The hands were trained that

way. My friends weren't. I should have been watching in all four directions instead of just three. If I had seen the storm sooner, we would have had more time to find shelter.

I looked at the sky again and tightened the cinches on our saddles. The storm was coming fast. There was another reason I was angry. If the storm had been coming from behind us, there might have been some chance of staying ahead of it long enough to reach the ranch. This storm was covering the northern sky and coming south, with the worst part directly north of us. I reckoned the ranch must have been getting drenched right about then.

As I helped Tom rinse our plates in the creek, I heard the first rumble of thunder. I knew Ma and Grandma would be worried about us. "Please, God, don't let them embarrass me by sending help."

"What?" Tom asked.

"Oh, nothing," I replied. "I didn't know I was talking out loud."

"Who were you talking to?" he asked.

"I was praying," I answered.

"You talk to God the same way you talk to people," he commented. "Don't you feel silly talking to Someone you can't see?"

"No, I don't—and I'll tell you why as soon as we find some shelter." This was the chance I was looking for to share my faith, and I wanted to hang onto it.

"Are we in danger?" he asked.

"Not that I know of," I said.

"That storm looks bad," Tom said.

"That storm *is* bad," I responded, shaking the water from the plates I held. "That's why we'd better light a shuck for some kind of shelter. Come on!"

Our picnic was over, and our afternoon of exploring had been ruined. Right there was the third reason I was angry.

"What are we going to do?" Esther asked. We were mounted and ready to go.

"We're going to get very, very wet," said Jasper. He took off his hat, then replaced it, slipping the leather stampede string under his chin. Esther and I followed his example, but Tom was wearing a dude's hat that didn't have a stampede string. Taking off my bandana, I handed it to him.

"Throw this over your hat and tie it under your chin," I said.

"Do I have to?" Tom asked. "I'll look really silly, and besides, there's hardly any wind."

"Tie on your hat or kiss it good-bye," I snapped.

Esther glanced at me. I took a deep breath and then turned to Tom. "The wind isn't bad now," I said, "but it will be. You may look silly with your hat tied on, but I reckon you'll look a heap sillier chasing it across the prairie after the wind snatches it off your head and runs away with it."

When I looked back at Esther, she was smiling.

Without speaking, she mouthed the words, "Thank you."

Right then the worst part of that anger in me got on its horse, tipped its hat and rode out of town. I was glad to see it go. I had more important things to tend to.

"The way I see it," I said, "we have two choices."

"What are they?" asked Jasper.

"I think he's getting ready to tell us," said Tom.

"Well? Go ahead; we ain't got all day. There's a storm coming, you know," said Jasper.

"I reckon that storm will be here in less than an hour. We need to find a place to hole up until it blows over. We didn't see a place on the ride here. The only other time I rode this way, I was east of here. I didn't come this far south, but I didn't see any shelter where I was. We can swing northwest. By riding toward the storm, we'd only have half an hour at the most before the storm hit. We wouldn't be riding straight toward the ranch, but we wouldn't be getting any farther away either."

"What's our second choice?" asked Esther.

"We'd keep going the way we were headed," I replied.

"Farther away from the ranch?" asked Jasper. "That don't make sense."

"It would give us more time to find shelter, wouldn't it?" asked Tom. "Why can't we ride back the way we came and go through the storm? I've gotten wet before, and besides, we have these slickers. A little rain won't hurt us."

"No, it won't. A little lightning might, though." I told them about the lightning-struck cows Grandpa and I had found.

"I've heard that there are some caves northwest of here," said Esther.

"There's a line shack up here somewhere too, but it could be anywhere," I said.

"We need to do something quickly," Esther said. "What do you think we should do?"

"I think we should pray," I answered. I felt a knot forming in my stomach. I knew the others were depending on me. "But let's ride northwest while we're praying."

CHAPTER FIVE

I had another reason for wanting to ride northwest. I had reckoned us to be about dead center in the path of the storm. I hoped we could move out of its path a bit by riding northwest.

The idea was a good one, but it didn't work. We rode at a fast trot, and that storm kept coming straight at us.

In front of us the whole sky was black. Lightning spread across the sky like fiery golden spider webs. We felt as well as heard the rumbling thunder.

The wind hit us first. I was riding in front of the others, leaning forward and looking for shelter. That wall of wind straightened me up and almost lifted me out of my saddle. As I looked over my shoulder to see if the others were still mounted, I knew I had made a mistake. I should have made sure we put on our slickers before we mounted our horses. Now we would have to stop and dismount from animals that were jumpy because of the storm. We would have to unwrap our slickers from our bedrolls and put the slickers on in a strong wind. Then we would have to remount those spooked animals.

Tom was my main worry because he was nervous about riding anyway. His lips were pressed together,

and he was hanging onto the saddle horn and the
reins with both hands. *Please help us, Father,* I
prayed.

When I stopped Prince and dismounted, I ran to
Tom's horse first. After he had dismounted, I held
the reins while he struggled into his slicker.
Esther was doing the same for Jasper.

When I say that the wind was blowing hard,
Western folks will understand something that
other people won't. Back in Ohio we had seen
some wild storms with strong wind, but this wind
was different. It didn't come flying at us across
that open prairie empty-handed. That wind had
picked up bits of sand, rock and dried sagebrush.
It had plucked loose feathers, flower petals and
seeds and all kinds of tiny things. Then it had carried them across the prairie and was flinging
them at us as hard as it could.

I had been caught twice before in storms like
this one. Both times I had been close to the ranch
before the rain had come, and both times the
storm had been behind me. All I had to go on now
was what I had learned from listening to others. I
hoped that was going to be enough. I knew that
pulling our bandanas up to cover our mouths and
noses would keep out some of the grit, but my bandana was holding Tom's hat on.

I squinted at Jasper and Esther. Both had covered their faces. I don't know where she got them,
but Esther was holding out two more bandanas
toward me.

I don't pretend to know the cause of what happened next. It might have been Tom's slicker flapping in the wind as he tried to put it on. The wind might have slammed an angry bee against Tom's horse, or something might have hit her in the eye or blown into her ear. I only know that as I reached for those bandanas, Tom's horse reared. She jerked the reins from my hand and, with a high-pitched squeal, took off at a dead run.

"Stay here!" I shouted. As I swung my leg over the saddle, Prince was already galloping after Tom's horse. If that horse had been a faster one, I would have needed my lariat to catch her. Since she was old and not as fast as Prince, even without her rider, I was able to get ahead of her.

Leaning from my saddle, I grabbed one of the dangling reins and stopped her. As I circled in front of her, I caught the other one and headed back toward my friends. Although no harm had come to horse or rider, we had lost some of the little bit of time we had before the storm caught us.

By the time I reached my friends, Tom's horse had calmed down enough to let me help him into the saddle.

As we headed northwest again, I looked at the sky. We hadn't felt a drop of rain yet, but the knot in my stomach tightened. The black clouds were stampeding toward us like an angry herd. All four of us had our faces covered with bandanas up to our eyes. Our hats were pulled down as far as we could pull them, but the wind folded the brims back. Sand stung my eyes and forehead as I looked for some kind of a shelter.

We were crossing what looked like a large plain covered with sagebrush. To the right, I couldn't see anything but open space. To the left, at least two miles away I could see some low rocks or hills. *Please let us find shelter there,* I prayed.

I wanted to let the horses run; but knowing there were unseen dangers, I held Prince to a trot. The plain looked like a smooth, flat, open area, but I reckoned it probably wasn't. I had ridden other country like this. Prairie dog holes were always dangerous to a running horse. Although I'd never seen it happen, I knew that stepping in a hole could snap a horse's leg. I had heard stories about horses falling on their riders too. Sometimes a rider would be thrown clear but break an arm, a leg or maybe even his neck.

There was another danger to a running horse on a plain like this one. Much of the year this land was the way we had found it, rock hard and dried out. Rain didn't come often, but when it did come, it fell so hard that the ground couldn't absorb it, so a good bit of it ran off. Over the years that water had followed the same path each time the rain came, wearing away the dirt and making dry washes, or arroyos, deep gullies with steep walls and flat bottoms.

They're dry most of the time. The danger is that you can't see them until you're right on top of them. If a man's walking his horse, there's no problem. If he's riding hard, his horse might jump some of the smaller ones. Sooner or later, though, he'll come to a big one—and some of them are big enough to hide a house in—and he'll be in serious trouble.

I didn't want any of us to wind up in that kind of trouble.

I was riding with Esther on my right. Tom was behind me, and Jasper behind Esther. The thunder was getting louder and the lightning closer. Still the rain hadn't caught us.

Because the sky had turned so dark, we were only three hundred yards from the line shack when I saw it. Turning to the others, I yelled and pointed toward the shack.

Then the rain came.

If I hadn't seen the line shack before the rain started, I reckon we would have missed it. The

rain pounded us. Everything around us disappeared. I felt like I had ridden under a giant waterfall. I kept riding in the general direction of the line shack. After what seemed like hours, Prince stopped in front of a small corral beside the shack. Following the fence, I found the shack.

I turned and looked at a solid wall of rain. Cupping my hands around my mouth, I yelled to my friends. As I listened to the thunder and the pounding rain, I reckoned they'd be close enough to see me before they heard me.

Like a ghost, Esther appeared from out of that wall of rain. I slid from my saddle and helped her down. Taking the reins from her, I pointed toward the shack.

"Start a fire," I shouted. "Watch out for critters—especially rattlers! I'll take care of your horse and watch for the others." Esther nodded and ran toward the shack.

The corral was fenced on three sides. The fourth side was one end of the shack. Close to the middle of the front side of the corral was a gate. When I got to the gate, I tied Prince's reins to one of the fence rails. Then I led Esther's horse into the corral and removed the saddle and bridle and carried them to an open lean-to built on the end of the shack. Someone had sunk two posts about eight feet apart and had fastened a ten-foot rail across them. I threw the saddle over the rail to dry and hung the bridle on one of the pegs that stuck out of the shack's wall.

I ran back to Prince, untied him and led him through the gate and under the lean-to. Leaving his saddle on, I tied his reins to the rail and watched for Tom and Jasper. Esther's horse had followed me to the shelter of the lean-to. The two animals heard Jasper coming for three or four minutes before I spotted him. He was riding past the corral when Prince whinnied. Jasper's mule turned and trotted toward us. A few minutes later Jasper's saddle was hanging beside Esther's.

Hanging his bridle on a peg, he turned to face me. After pulling his soaked bandana down, he just looked at me with his eyes and mouth wide open. Then he swallowed hard and shouted, "I reckon we lost Tom."

CHAPTER SIX

The storm made talking too difficult. Thunder was exploding every two or three minutes. The lightning that came with it spooked the horses, causing them to squeal, snort and stomp around in the crowded lean-to. The wind was howling, and the rain was hammering on the roof.

Motioning for Jasper to follow, I ducked between the rails of the corral and ran to the door of the shack. Jasper and I burst through the doorway together, and I helped him force the door closed against the storm.

I had never been inside a line shack before; in fact, I had never even seen one from the outside. It reminded me of another shack, where Jeff Chastain and Rafe Alman had taken Ma and me after kidnapping us.

I shuddered as I looked around me.

Esther was adding kindling wood to a small fire blazing in the rusty, pot-bellied stove that stood in the middle of the shack's only room. Her slicker was hung over one of the two chairs that faced each other on either side of an old table that sat halfway between the stove and the right wall.

Against the left wall—the one with the lean-to attached to it—was a cot with no bedding on it.

The back wall was bare except for three shelves on the upper half. I reckoned they were about four feet long. Two of them were empty, but the third one had several tins and a lantern on it. The whole room must have been between twelve and fifteen feet square. The ceiling sloped from eight feet on the right to seven feet on the other side.

Esther closed the stove door and turned to face us. She had been smiling, but she stopped when she saw only two of us. "Where's Tom?" She had spoken so softly that I had barely heard her over the drumming of the rain on the roof. I turned to Jasper. He stood there, his eyes bulging, water dripping from his hat brim and his slicker.

"We...we was together until that big flash of lightning right before you saw me," he said. "Tom's

horse took off at a dead run in the direction we
were heading. I started after him, but when I saw
you, I reckoned I'd better get some help. Now I've
wasted all this time, and...," Jasper choked back
a sob and wiped the back of his sleeve across
his eyes.

"You did the right thing, Jasper," Esther
assured him. "Drape your slicker over the other
chair and come stand here by the fire."

"I have to find Tom!" said Jasper, his eyes
bulging even more.

"I'll find him," I stated. I stepped to the door
and put my hand on his shoulder. "Esther's right;
you did the right thing. I'll find Tom. You two
stay here."

"Can't I help?" asked Jasper.

"You sure can," I replied. "You can both pray,
and don't waste any time getting started." I pulled
the brim of my hat down, stepped outside and
closed the door behind me.

The rain was falling harder than ever. I ran
along the front of the shack and ducked under the
lean-to. While I checked the girth on Prince's saddle, I prayed aloud: "I'm scared, and I don't reckon
I can find Tom on my own. Pa is with You, and
Grandpa, Chad and the others are back at the
ranch. You're going to be the One riding with me."

Suddenly I remembered something Ma had
said on our stagecoach ride to Texas. When those
two polecats, Rafe Alman and Jeff Chastain, had
asked if we were traveling alone, she had told

them that her Father was traveling with us, talking about her Heavenly Father—and mine.

I led Prince out of the lean-to and swung into the saddle. The knot that had been forming in my stomach began to ease up a bit. "Let's go find Tom, Father," I prayed.

I rode in the direction we had been heading when we found the shack. I reckoned I still had about three hours of daylight left, but the rain was making me mosey along when I wanted to gallop. Seeing only about five or six yards in front of me, I yelled Tom's name every two minutes or so, but the storm was so noisy that he would have had to have been riding beside me to hear or be heard.

I lost track of time and distance as I tried to keep my bearings. I'd heard of men who had been caught in storms and had ridden in circles until they had either been rescued or had died.

Then, as suddenly as it had started, the storm broke. First the rain stopped; then the sky began to clear. As I watched, the dark clouds raced away, taking the rain, thunder and lightning with them.

As soon as the breeze had dried my slicker, I dismounted, took it off and put it back into my bedroll. "Thanks, Father," I said. "Things should be a bit easier now."

Back in the saddle, I stood in the stirrups and looked in every direction. Far off to my left something was moving. It was too far away to be certain, but I thought it might be a horse.

Pointing Prince in that direction, I nudged him

into a gallop. My heart was pounding. If I had found Tom's horse, Tom wouldn't be far away.

I reined Prince in when I had gotten close enough to see that it was only a white-tailed deer. Turning back to the direction I had been riding, I gave Prince his head, and he again began to gallop across the prairie.

We had crossed some arroyos and ridden around several others, but I had seen no sign of Tom anywhere. I reckoned I had better than two hours of daylight left as I rode up to the biggest arroyo we'd found yet. Twenty feet wide and between fifteen and twenty feet deep, it stretched in both directions as far as I could see.

"Which way, Father?" I asked aloud. "I don't

have enough daylight to look in both directions." A muddy stream that looked to be three feet wide flowed from the south along the arroyo's bottom. As I watched the current carrying bits of cactus, weeds, flowers, butterflies and even a dead bird, I saw something larger floating toward me.

At first it looked like a large tortoise, half floating, half crawling over the rocks and brush that lay in the path of the stream. Curious, I turned Prince, and he began to mosey along the rim of the arroyo in that direction. When I realized what the object was, I felt sick. It wasn't a tortoise or an armadillo or any other animal. It was Tom's hat!

CHAPTER SEVEN

I had no way of knowing how long that hat had been floating or how far it had come. My first thought was that I should ride upstream as fast as I could until I found Tom. Instead, I stopped to pray. Some would reckon me to be somewhere between a saint and an angel for being so spiritual at such a hard time. I prayed because I was plumb scared.

Then I sat and thought for a spell. That hat might not be Tom's. I sure didn't want it to be. Other people in Texas—even two or three in White Rock—wore hats like that one. The wind could have blown a hat like that for miles across the prairie and into that arroyo.

I shook myself. Nobody was fool enough to believe a stretch like that.

Another more believable chance was that Tom's hat had blown off in the storm and fallen into the arroyo. The fact that Tom's hat was down there didn't guarantee that he was.

There was still the question of how long that hat had been floating. I let Prince walk along the edge of the arroyo, moving upstream. The arroyo stretched in front of me like a giant sidewinder, so long that I couldn't see its head. Above it the storm reminded me of a huge, black Phantom walking slowly away but turning his head to snarl at me every few minutes.

I turned my attention back to the bottom of the arroyo and nudged Prince into a trot. I was sure I had less than two hours of daylight. Every hundred yards or so I called Tom's name, then listened for an answer, but I heard nothing. Following the twists and turns of the arroyo, I could never see very far ahead. Then I rounded a sharp bend and found myself looking down on the two still forms lying on the edge of that stream at the bottom.

I knew from the way Prince was acting that either Tom or his horse—or maybe both—were dead. I swallowed hard. Tom wasn't born again. *Please don't let him be dead,* I prayed.

Prince snorted and sidestepped while I patted his neck to calm him down. I needed someone to calm me too. Then the words popped into my head: *"What time I am afraid, I will trust in thee."* I reckoned this was sure enough a time when I was afraid.

Prince stood still. I took a deep breath and let it out slowly. "I'm trusting, Father," I said aloud. "Help me."

I could still see the deep ruts in the bank where Tom's horse had tried to regain her footing after the edge had broken away. I would have to go down several yards downstream from Tom. I reckoned getting down wouldn't be a problem. The steep, muddy bank of that arroyo would let me slide down. The problem was going to be getting back up that bank again, especially if Tom was hurt too badly to walk or he was—"Stop it!" I yelled.

Prince snorted and jumped. I leaned forward and patted his neck again. "Sorry, pardner," I whispered. "What I meant was, 'What time I am afraid, I will trust in thee.'"

"I reckon I'm going to have to put some trust in you too, Prince," I said as I stepped to the ground, leaving Prince a safe distance from the edge. First, I took a pair of leather gloves from one of my saddlebags. Then, taking my lariat from my saddle, I made a loop on one end and slipped it around the saddle horn. "Stay put," I said, stepping to the edge of the arroyo and tossing the other end of the coiled lariat over the bank.

Letting the wet rope slip through my gloved hands, I walked backwards down the steep, muddy bank until I was holding the end of my lariat. I let go and dropped the last foot or so to the bottom. Tom's horse was dead for certain. I could see as I ran toward her that, although most of her body lay on the solid ground, the muddy stream covered her mouth and nostrils.

Then I stopped. For a few seconds I stood there, afraid of what I might find on the other side of that horse. From the top of the arroyo, I had been able to see that Tom was pinned under it just clear of the stream, but nothing more. Falling into the arroyo could have been enough to kill Tom; having over a thousand pounds of horseflesh land on top of him couldn't have helped his chances of living.

I shook myself and closed my eyes. *"What time I am afraid, I will trust in thee."* Opening my eyes, I stepped around the horse's body. Tom was lying on his back. Both of his legs were pinned under the horse from the thigh down. His eyes were closed, and he wasn't moving.

I knelt beside him and pulled the glove from my right hand. Holding my breath, I reached out and put the back of my hand to the right side of his face. Tom opened his eyes, sat up and, grabbing my arm, began to scream! Just in case you're wondering, I screamed too.

When we had settled down a bit, I asked, "Are you hurt bad?"

"I...I don't think so," he answered. "I can't move

my legs, and I'm scratched and bruised everywhere, but I don't think anything is broken. I'm really sorry about your horse. I'll figure out a way to pay your ma for her."

"You're not paying for this horse. If you're not hurt, why were you unconscious? If you're not in pain, why did you scream?"

"I was asleep," he replied. Then he began to laugh. "And I was having a nightmare that some Indians had found me here and were going to scalp me! When I felt your hand and woke up, I guess I thought you were one of them."

"I'm glad you weren't armed," I sighed. "You might have shot me."

"Can you get me out of here?" he asked.

"Yes, and the sooner the better," I answered. "We're burning daylight. I don't reckon we're going to move this horse, so we'll have to dig you out. Let me see what I can find to use for a shovel."

I scouted around until I found a sturdy branch about three feet long and as big around as my arm. Starting about a foot from the horse and the same distance from Tom's leg, I began to dig. The stick slid into the soft wet dirt with no trouble, but I had to use my hands to scoop it from under the horse.

When the hole was finally deep enough for me to feel Tom's boot, I stopped to catch my breath. I wiped my sweaty face on my bandana and stayed there on my knees for a minute to catch my breath. Then I crawled around Tom and started on the other side.

"I wish I could help," Tom said.

"Try to move your legs once in a while and let me know when you feel them come loose," I replied.

"I can already move my left leg a little," he said.

I had dug as far as Tom's right knee when I hit a rock. I widened and deepened the hole, but I couldn't get around it.

"I need Your help," I said.

"I don't know what I can do," Tom replied.

"Sorry, pard, I wasn't talking to you. I reckon I didn't know I was talking out loud."

"You're not going loco, are you?" Tom asked, looking around. "There's no one else here...oh, praying again, aren't you?"

I agreed I was praying. "I have to get around this rock to free your leg."

I looked around at the shadows that had begun to cover the arroyo. Picking up the stick again, I began to dig. I tunneled under the rock, hoping that it would settle enough to free Tom's leg. Sweat blinded me, and my arms ached. Using the stick, I tried to pry the rock loose. I was jumping on the stick with both feet when it snapped. I fell, landing on my back beside Tom.

I stayed there until I had caught my breath. "Now I have to find another stick," I said. I sat up and then rolled onto my hands and knees.

As I started to get to my feet, Tom spoke. "I think you'd better hurry." He nodded toward the horse. The holes on both sides of his legs had filled with water. From where we were we could see about 150 yards up the arroyo because the curves were small. During the time that I had been digging, the little stream had doubled its width and increased its speed.

Looking at the sky in the direction the water was coming from, I felt sick.

Stepping over Tom, I knelt in the water and began to dig as fast as I could. Since the water was almost to Tom's waist, I had to feel instead of see what I was doing. I felt along his leg until I found the cuff of his pants. Grabbing it with both hands, I threw my whole body backwards.

"It moved!" Tom cried. "Try again!"

This time when I threw myself backwards, Tom's leg came free; and I landed on my back in the cold water. I rolled over and crawled back to the horse. My job was harder now because I had to reach over Tom's left leg to dig. Also, I reckoned Tom must have landed with his legs spread, because I couldn't feel anything but dirt. Because of my awkward position, I could only dig with my left hand.

I handed Tom my Stetson and laid my head on his shoulder as I dug. Lying in that position left me looking into Tom's pale face. His teeth were chattering, and he looked mighty scared. I reckoned if I could strike up a conversation with him, we'd pass the time and both stay calm. Well, although the idea seemed like a good one at the time, I reckoned wrong.

CHAPTER EIGHT

"Don't worry, pard; I'll have you out of here in no time," I assured him. *"What time I am afraid, I will trust in thee,"* I thought.

I reckoned there wasn't a chance we could get back to that line shack before dark. I wasn't sure how far I had ridden in the storm before I found the arroyo, but I knew I had come more than a mile—probably closer to two.

Getting back was going to be a slow business because only one of us would be riding. Prince could probably carry both of us for that short distance, but he had never been ridden double before. And I doubted he'd be excited about trying something new.

In daylight, finding the shack would be simple. We'd be able to see it sticking up from that wide, open plain. In the dark, we could ride within twenty yards of it and not even know it was there unless one of the animals made some noise. I didn't think there was enough dry wood to keep a fire burning long. I doubted that there had been enough coal oil to keep the lantern burning any length of time.

"This water is rising fast," Tom said.

My numb fingers brushed against something

solid. "I've found your other leg! We'll be out of here pronto."

"Who's Pronto?" asked Tom.

"Sorry," I said, laughing and trying to keep my teeth from chattering. "That's Mexican for 'in a hurry.'"

"What if you can't get me out in time?" he whispered. Tears ran from the corners of his eyes. "I don't want to die, Arty."

My arm ached so badly I wanted to scream, but I clawed as fast as I could at the mud and stones that were packed around his leg. "You're not going to die from a little cold water!" I assured him.

"That's just it," said Tom. He swallowed hard. "I know I'm a dude, and I don't know half of what you've learned about tracking and shooting and that kind of stuff. Most of what I know comes from books."

I had uncovered Tom's pant cuff, but I was in a bad position to pull. After tugging on it twice and feeling no movement, I went back to digging.

"I've read about these arroyos, and I've heard a few people talking about them too," he continued. "I've been watching that storm, Arty. Unless I miss my guess, it's still raining hard further up this arroyo."

"Better there than here," I said. I pulled again on his pant leg, but I still felt no movement. I wondered how much longer I could keep digging.

"The ground is too hard and dry to absorb so

much rain," Tom commented. "The water is already touching the back of my head."

"Well, pard, if you're worried about it messing up your hair, you just—"

"Listen to me!" he screamed. He took a deep breath. I knew he was trying hard not to cry. He sniffed twice, then said quietly, "All that rain is running into the upper end of this arroyo. Any minute now a wall of water will come roaring down through here, sweeping away this dead horse and drowning both of us."

"I can remember times when you've been better company." I was smiling as I said it, but I couldn't stop my tears. I knew he was right.

"Leave me," Tom said.

I pulled hard on his cuff, and his leg moved a couple of inches. "You're almost free!" I sobbed.

"It's too late!" Tom replied. "Get out of here!"

"I'm not leaving you," I told him, trying to calm down. "Arty the Kid never abandons a member of his gang." As I jerked on his cuff, I screamed with each jerk. Suddenly Tom's leg pulled free. "I got you! Let's get out of here!"

I don't know how long I had been lying in that cold water, but I tried twice to stand up and fell both times. On the third try I stayed up, but I had to stomp around to get my legs back. When I grabbed Tom under the arms, I was so weak I could barely pull him clear of the water.

"Arty, I can't even feel my legs," Tom said. "You have to go!"

"Not without you," I replied.

"I can't walk!" he screamed.

"Then I reckon I'll have to drag you, because you're too heavy to carry. You should've skipped that last piece of johnnycake." This time I smiled.

We were both cold and wet, but Tom was free, and I thought we'd be out of the arroyo in something less than fifteen minutes. I might even have time to come back for the saddle and bridle from Tom's horse. Tom didn't share my good feeling.

Dragging him across the bottom of the arroyo took all of fifteen minutes because I had to keep stopping to rest every few yards. By the time we had reached the foot of the bank, I was exhausted. By then Tom was able to stand, as long as he hung onto me. I helped him take a few wobbly steps, then we both sat down on a boulder.

"Let's catch our breath; then we'll climb the bank."

"I can't climb the bank unless I get my legs back," groaned Tom. "Let me lean on you and walk around for a while."

For ten minutes or more, we walked back and forth between two boulders, stopping at each one so Tom could rest. "I think I'm ready to try now," he said.

"Good! Sit here and rest a minute. I'm going to fetch the saddle and bridle from your horse. Maybe we can figure a way to get them out of here."

The sun had dropped far enough to put the

whole arroyo in shadow, and I felt a chill as I bent over the dead horse. Thunder rumbled far away. It kept on rumbling, getting louder and louder. When I felt the ground shaking, I knew the sound wasn't thunder. I ran for the bank, shouting as loudly as I could, "Climb, Tom! Climb!"

As I ran around boulders and jumped over brush and smaller rocks, everything seemed to happen in slow motion. I saw Tom jump for the end of my lariat and miss, falling onto his hands and knees. He struggled to his feet and jumped again. This time he caught the end of the lariat with his right hand and swung himself sideways, grabbing it with his left hand too.

Bracing his feet against the muddy bank, Tom

began to climb the rope. I was five or six steps away when suddenly, like a big catfish that had taken the bait, Tom was pulled up the bank and over the rim. The lariat disappeared with him.

Prince must have spooked and run. In less than a minute I realized that the rumble had turned to a roar. I turned to look up the arroyo. A wall of water ten feet high and reaching from bank to bank was roaring toward me. I raised my arms and screamed. Something jerked me off my feet. The wall of water slammed into me, and everything went black.

CHAPTER NINE

"Breathe, Arty! Breathe!" Esther whispered from somewhere in the blackness.

I could hear her voice close to me, but I couldn't see her. I couldn't see anything. Soaked to the skin, I was lying facedown. Something heavy pushed on my back, eased off, then pushed again. My whole body hurt. When the next push came, I groaned.

"He's alive!" exclaimed Tom.

"Praise God!" said Esther.

"Are you really there?" I asked.

"He's blind!" answered Jasper.

I started to laugh but gritted my teeth and groaned at what felt like a horse kicking me in the ribs. I opened my eyes but still couldn't see. Turning my head just a little, I saw a star. Night had come. My left cheek was resting on some kind of cloth. The rest of me was stretched on the ground, and someone was sitting on my back.

"I can't move," I whispered.

"He's parallel!" said Jasper.

"You mean paralyzed," Tom said.

"He is?" asked Jasper.

"No," Tom replied, "I was just—"

"Will whoever's sitting on me please get off," I requested wearily.

"Oh, sorry, Arty," said Tom. "I was pumping the water out of you. I got so excited when you came around that I forgot where I was!"

As soon as Tom had moved, I rolled onto my back. I couldn't stop the groan that slipped past my gritted teeth. When I raised myself on one elbow, the worst pain I'd ever felt ripped through my right side. Gritted teeth or not, I screamed and fell back; but I didn't feel the ground when I hit it.

The next time I opened my eyes, I was very cold and on my back, looking at a sky full of stars. I couldn't see their faces, but I saw the dim outlines of Jasper, Tom and Esther, all sitting around me on the ground. Someone was crying quietly.

"Welcome back," said Esther. "We need to get you back to the line shack, but the trip won't be much fun."

"Lying here on the ground in wet clothes is no picnic," I said, trying not to let my teeth chatter. "I'm sorry to be so much trouble, Esther. I hate to tell you this, but I don't reckon I know exactly where that shack is from here."

"I do," she said. I couldn't see her face in the darkness, but I knew she was smiling. "All you have to do is stay in the saddle till we get there. It's a little over a mile, but the ground is flat and smooth."

"Flat and smooth enough that you could just slip a loop under my arms and drag me?" I asked.

"No," she replied, laughing. "We'd ruin your clothes, and you don't have any others with you. We need to get you out of those wet duds and dry them while you get warm."

"*We?*" I asked. I was glad for the darkness, because I could feel myself blushing. "I reckon I can take my own clothes off," I told her. "I'm not stove up that badly."

"Yes, you are," she whispered.

"No, I'm not," I argued.

"Then get up and get on Prince," she commanded. I still couldn't see her face, but I could hear the irritation in her voice.

"I will," I said. I sat up, fighting the urge to scream. I thought I was going to black out again, but my head cleared this time. Putting my hand to the back of my aching head, I felt a large knot. The stiffness of the hair around it told me that there was also dried blood from a cut. I tried rolling over, first to one side and then to the other, so I could get to my feet. The pain in my side was too bad. I sat there, trying to think of a way out. If there was one, I couldn't find it.

Esther just stood beside me, waiting. Prince whinnied softly in the darkness. A few seconds later Tom appeared like a shadow and led him close to me. Jasper was right behind him with his mule and Esther's horse.

"What's the plan?" asked Tom.

"We're heading back to the line shack," I answered. "You can ride double with Esther because her horse is used to having one of her sisters behind the saddle. Jasper and I will follow you two on our mounts."

"Sounds good to me," Tom replied. "I want to get out of these wet clothes and get close to a fire. You have to be freezing too, Arty. Can you ride?"

"I reckon I might need a hand getting into the saddle," I said.

Even though I couldn't have seen her face in the dark, I didn't look at Esther. Without saying a word, she took the reins of our mounts and let Jasper and Tom help me. I only groaned once while they helped me to my feet. Then I noticed that I had lost my right boot as well as my hat. When they half-lifted me into the saddle, the pain in my side made me scream. I scared Prince, making him snort and prance enough that I almost fell off.

Now, I'm smart enough at book learning to know that every mile is exactly the same length. I rode back weeks later to check the distance, and it really was within shouting distance of a mile from the arroyo to the shack. That night I would have sworn that we rode closer to five miles. As smooth-gaited as Prince is, I felt as if someone were banging my side like a bass drum on the Fourth of July all the way.

God's mercy kept me from falling out of the saddle at least a dozen times. Worried as they were about me, I reckon my friends would have worried a good bit more had we been riding by daylight. Then they could have seen what was going on. In the dark, only I knew what was happening, and that was bad enough.

I reckon I must have been in pretty bad shape by the time we got to the shack. I don't remember being helped down from Prince's back or going inside. When I woke up on the cot in the shack, I was lying between some blankets, warm and dry. I

could hear the fire crackling and smell the coffee. I opened my eyes and saw Jasper in the firelight of the open stove hanging Tom's clothes on a makeshift clothesline. Tom was sitting on the floor close to the stove wrapped in a blanket and sipping something hot—tea, I reckoned.

"This is dry, Tom," said Jasper, handing him a shirt.

"Thanks."

Jasper sat cross-legged beside Tom with a cup of coffee. "Want me to hold that while you put your shirt on?"

Tom handed his cup to Jasper and pulled the shirt on over his head. Letting the blanket slip to the floor, he stood, tucked his shirt into his pants and pulled his suspenders over his shoulders. Then he folded the blanket and laid it on the other side of him. He motioned for Esther, who came from the shadows to sit on the blanket.

"Give her that tea, Jasper," Tom said. "I'll make another cup."

Smiling, I lay still and began to drift off to sleep. My side didn't hurt as much when I wasn't moving. I was almost asleep when a very disturbing thought stomped into my head, wearing boots and jangling spurs. I was warm and dry already.

Slowly I took the edge of the blanket between the thumb and trigger finger of each hand and looked toward the stove to make sure no one had noticed that I was awake. Tucking my chin against my chest, I lifted the blanket. Sure enough, I was dressed in my warm, dry clothes. I must have made a noise because when I looked toward the stove again, all three of my friends were looking at me.

"We dried your clothes first," Tom said, "while Esther waited outside."

"How long did it take to...how long was she out there in the dark by herself?" I asked.

"Well, this isn't the fastest way to dry clothes,"

replied Jasper. "She had to wait out there for almost—"

"Not all that long," broke in Esther. "I stayed close to the door. My being inside would hardly have been proper, would it?"

I was angry that she had been outside alone in the dark for well over an hour because of me. I wanted to argue with her, but I knew she was right.

CHAPTER TEN

In the middle of the night, I was lying on a cot in a line shack, miles from home. Ma, Grandma and Grandpa and the hands had to be mighty worried about us, ready to start looking for us at daybreak.

My head had never hurt the way it was hurting right then. My side felt as if someone had run a herd of cattle over me. Breathing hurt while I was lying still, and I had to ride all the way home on Prince before I could get Doc O'Leary to take a look at me. Otherwise, everything was just dandy!

I tried to sit up, but the pain in my side made me want to scream. "Please help me," I prayed. "I'm responsible for my friends. Help me get them out of this mess."

"Why? You certainly didn't get us into it," Esther whispered.

I opened my eyes to find her kneeling beside the cot. I reckoned I must have been praying out loud.

She smiled and shook her head. "I reckon that, even without Arty the Kid to lead us, the three of us can probably keep from burning the shack down before help gets here," she said. "You just rest easy. Do you feel like talking?"

"No," I replied, "but I feel like listening. The last thing I recollect from being in that arroyo is

something jerking me off my feet just before
that wall of water hit me. Then a few minutes later
I was up on the rim with Tom bouncing on my back.
What happened during those few minutes that I
blacked out?"

"Would you like some coffee?" she asked. When
I said yes, Esther helped me raise my head and
shoulders. I gritted my teeth and held my breath
until she had wedged a bedroll behind me. She
stood, and brushing the dust from her riding skirt,
she looked over her shoulder toward the fire. "The
boys are asleep. I'm going to get some tea and put
some more wood in the stove. Then we can talk."

A few minutes later with both hands she held
out a cup of steaming coffee. Then she set a chair
beside the cot. She sat down, holding her
cup in both hands, staring into it without saying
anything.

"Esther?" I said.

She shuddered, then looked at me. "I'm sorry.
What do you want to know?"

"Everything," I replied. "How much could have
happened in the few minutes that I was out?" I
could only get comfortable, propped up the way I
was, by staying on my back. Closing my eyes, I
sipped my coffee and listened.

"When the storm broke," Esther said softly, "I
supposed Jasper and I might help you either in
finding Tom or in bringing him back if he had been
hurt. By then I knew we'd have no trouble finding
the cabin again. With the weather clear, I thought

we'd be able to find you either by seeing you or by picking up your trail from where you were when the rain stopped." She paused, and without looking, I knew she was sipping her tea.

"We picked up your tracks not far from the

arroyo," she continued. "A quarter of an hour later, we spotted Prince standing by the arroyo about two hundred yards ahead of us. We sure were glad to see him, but he didn't pay us any mind. He was looking the other direction. As we rode closer, we saw the rope tied to his saddle horn. Since it was stretched tight, we figured someone was on the other end of it."

As Esther stopped to sip more tea, I opened my eyes. I had finished my coffee, so she set my empty cup on the floor.

"Do you want to rest?" she asked. "What I have to say will keep."

"No," I said. "Go on. I want to find out what I missed."

"Jasper led Prince away from the arroyo, and I helped Tom over the edge. Then I saw the water. Jasper had Prince back by then. I was ready to throw you a loop when Tom told me your lariat didn't reach the bottom. I grabbed Jasper's lariat and told him to tie one end to the end of yours after I'd made a loop in the other. I knew I'd only get one chance, so I whispered a prayer and tossed my loop. You saw it coming and raised your arms to guide it. I jerked it taut as soon as it had passed your shoulders."

I felt the hair on the back of my neck stand up. As much as it hurt me to turn my head, I managed. "Esther," I said, "I never saw you or that rope. I thought I'd reached the end of my trail. I lifted my arms because...well, because...I reckon I don't know why. I was scared, and I think I was praying. I..." I stopped when I saw her face. She looked pale in the shadows of the fire. "Are you all right?" I asked.

"Yes," she whispered. She shuddered again, then continued. "I snugged the line as much as I could. Jasper started Prince again, but there wasn't enough time to take up all the slack between Prince and me. Then the water hit you."

As I sat up, the pain made me dizzy. Gritting my teeth and closing my eyes, I waited. My stomach was sick for a few minutes, but the feeling passed, and my coffee stayed put. When I could talk, I asked, "What happened out there? I blacked out for more than a few minutes, didn't I?"

Esther had bowed her head, and her reply was

so soft that I couldn't understand her. When her shoulders moved and she sniffed, I realized she was crying.

The fire flared up as Tom opened the door and threw a few more chips on it. "Lucky for us that someone stacked cow chips and some dead wood in the lean-to," he said. Standing behind Esther, he put his hands on her shoulders. "I've been awake for a few minutes, and I couldn't help hearing what you two have been talking about. Do you want me to take over, Esther?"

When she nodded her head, Tom continued: "Jasper and I were leading Prince away from the arroyo to tighten the rope. When I realized that the water was going to hit you, I was afraid the force would break the cinch or snap off the saddle horn. I grabbed the rope in the middle, hoping to take enough of the force to let Prince pull you out of the arroyo. Esther had the same idea, I guess, but she was too close to the edge. She had wrapped the rope around her hands to keep it from slipping. When the flood swept you down the arroyo, the rope tightened and pulled Esther over the edge."

When Tom paused, I realized that I had been holding my breath.

"They pulled me back over the edge, Arty; I'm fine!" Esther assured me.

I felt sick and cold. "Let me see your hands," I whispered.

"Arty, I'm fine. I was wearing gloves. I just lost my footing and—"

"Show me your hands!" I demanded.

Slowly she held them out to me, palms up. I started to gag when I saw them. Taking a deep breath, I reached out with my right hand. Esther rested one of her hands in mine. In the dim firelight I couldn't see the bruises; but I saw the swelling where the lariat had pulled tight, cutting off the circulation while she had hung over the arroyo. I didn't care who saw; I cried.

Esther was still crying. She knelt beside that old cot and took my face in her two swollen hands. Leaning close to me, she whispered, "After that awful wall of water hit you, we pulled you out of the arroyo."

"She wouldn't let me even look at her hands until she was sure you were all right," Tom said. "They're bruised badly, but I don't think anything's broken. Her gloves protected her."

"You were just lying there," said Esther. "We thought you were dead." She let her puffy hands slide down my face, then covered her own face with them. Tom walked back to the stove and closed the door.

I listened to the night wind for a while, then I reckon I just drifted off to sleep. I dreamed about our picnic in that beautiful valley. The four of us were chasing each other and laughing. All of a sudden we came to an arroyo that was so deep we couldn't see the bottom of it. I stopped, but my three friends went over the edge. As I watched them tumble over and over, I screamed. I was screaming when I woke up and found Esther still beside the cot.

CHAPTER ELEVEN

That night seemed to last forever. I kept dozing off, but I couldn't stay asleep. Sometimes in my sleep I moved, and the pain in my side jerked me awake. At times the nightmare about the valley came again, and I woke up screaming or crying—or both.

Twice I had a different nightmare. I was back in the arroyo watching someone pull the lariat over the rim and out of sight. When I turned and saw the wall of water roaring toward me, I ran. My feet kept getting tangled in brush and prickly pear. As the water caught up with me, the arroyo bottom turned to deep, sticky mud, the way the streets in White Rock do after a really heavy rain.

The mud sucked at my boots until it pulled them off, socks and all. Barefooted, I kept running—or trying to run. The wall of water thundered right behind me. When I looked over my shoulder, it was so high I couldn't see the top of it. It carried whole trees, Grandma and Grandpa's covered wagon, two lightning-struck cows, the line shack and a bunch of other stuff it had picked up.

Then I was at the box end of Coyote Canyon with no place to go. The lariat was hanging there, but just as I reached for it, Rafe Alman and Jeff Chastain pulled it up the canyon wall. Both times that I had the nightmare, they were leaning over the rim of the arroyo laughing at me, just before I woke up.

Finally I could see a patch of gray through the small window. Sunup couldn't be far off. Esther brought me some more coffee and a chunk of sourdough bread for breakfast.

An eerie feeling overtook me, but I couldn't quite put my finger on it.

Following Chad's training, I closed my eyes and listened. There was no sound besides the wind. All of a sudden I knew what was wrong. "Check the horses," I said to Tom.

Tom tore out the door. When he came back, his face told the story before he spoke. "They got loose! They're gone!"

I needed a minute or two to calm down. I was really angry, and I wanted to think for a minute before I said anything that I'd be sorry for later. Esther had taught me that much.

The way things worked out, God gave me more than a minute to think. Ten minutes had passed before the pain in my side and the sickness in my stomach had settled enough for me to talk. I was flat on my back again, staring at the ceiling when I spoke.

"Who put the horses in the corral when we got back here last night?" I asked, gritting my teeth. The three of them were so quiet for so long that I was beginning to wonder if they had sneaked out of the shack.

Finally Jasper answered in a whisper so low I could hardly hear him: "I fastened the gate, Arty...I know I did. I was tired, but—"

"Check the gate, Tom," I said. I heard Tom cross the floor of the shack. The door creaked open and then closed behind him.

"I fastened the gate, Arty," Jasper said.

"We'll see about that, won't we?" I replied. I was trying not to be too hard on Jasper. I was sure he hadn't *meant* to leave the gate open; but he was...well, he was Jasper.

When Tom came back in, he didn't say anything. I knew he'd found the gate unfastened. I wanted to scream at Jasper. I wanted to tell him that because of his carelessness we were stuck in this shack until someone found us. Even when some of the hands did find us, we'd have to wait while they rode back to the ranch to get the buckboard or some more horses.

When I heard a sniff, I knew without looking that Jasper was crying. I reckoned he was crying because he knew I didn't believe him. No one said anything. Someone went outside. I knew Jasper wouldn't lie to me. I reckoned I needed to let him know.

"Jasper?" I said. He didn't say anything, but he stepped to the side of the cot. "If you say you fastened the gate, pard, I believe you. I'm sorry I doubted you at first. I reckon the pain must have fogged my brain for a minute."

For a bit Jasper just stood there. "Thanks, Arty," he said.

Whoever had left the shack came back in and walked over to the cot. I turned my head just enough to see Esther's face.

"Jasper did fasten the gate last night," she said softly.

"How do you know?" I asked.

"Whoever stole our animals saddled and bridled them first," she replied.

I might have screamed because someone had stolen Prince. Maybe I screamed because I knew that we were stranded in that shack until someone found us. I reckon I might have screamed because when Esther told me about the horses, I had tried to sit up. Whatever the reason, I screamed—long and loud. I learned right then that a fellow who probably has broken ribs shouldn't scream.

Prince was gone! I'd get him back, though, and some thieving rustler would pay. Most times horse thieves were strung up from the nearest tree when they were caught.

As upset as I was about that news, I was most thankful that I had believed Jasper. I tried to think, but my screaming had kicked the pounding in my head from a trot to a gallop.

I knew that riders were already out looking for us. And I knew that sooner or later, they were bound to find us. What I needed to do was to try to make us easier to find.

They would start looking somewhere near that valley where we had had our picnic. The rain would have washed away every sign of us, but somehow Chad would figure out that we'd been there. Then he'd just stand in the middle of that valley, looking around, listening and smelling the air. Then he'd mount up and ride off—more than likely heading the same way we had ridden.

I had a lot of trust in Chad and the other hands, but he had taught me to do whatever I could to help someone who was looking if I wanted him to find me. I knew there were things that we should do, but I couldn't clear my head enough to remember what they were.

Bang! Bang! Bang! Someone had fired three shots just outside the door of the shack. Three shots were the signal for help to come. The hands would hear the signal and find us pronto!

"Esther," I said, "tell Jasper he did a good thing."

"What did I do?" asked Jasper. He was standing beside me.

"How did a dude like Tom know about the signal?" I asked, surprised.

"What signal?" asked Tom.

The door opened and closed. Someone crossed the shack. I listened as someone ejected the empty shells from my six-gun, slid the cartridges from my gun belt into the empty chambers and slid the gun into the holster.

"Esther?"

She walked to the side of the cot. "Yes?"

"You fired those shots to let them know where we are? What about your hands? Are they—"

"We do want someone to find us, don't we?" she

questioned, raising her eyebrows.

"Well, yes, but I didn't expect...I mean, I didn't know that you...uh...."

"You didn't think a girl would be smart enough to think of signaling for help?" she asked, leaning over me and smiling.

"No. I mean, yes...I know how smart you are in book learning and all. I was just surprised that you knew...that you knew—"

"Cowboy stuff?" She laughed. "Arty, I was born on our ranch. Before I was old enough to go to school, I had learned a lot of what Chad has taught you. I needed to be able to take care of myself too. The signal for help was one of the first things I learned." She brushed my hair away from my eyes with the back of one bruised, swollen hand and smiled. "You rest, cowboy. Help is on the way."

CHAPTER TWELVE

As hard as I tried not to, I still drifted off to sleep again. Ma's voice woke me, and her worried face was the first thing I saw when I opened my eyes. She wasn't quite crying, but her eyes were watery.

"How bad are you hurt?" she asked.

"You mean how *badly*," I said, grinning.

"Tell me where you hurt most," she said, smiling down at me, "so I can poke you there." Then she stopped smiling. "What happened? How badly are you hurt? Can you move? Where are you hurt? Are you—"

Without letting her finish, I exclaimed, "Whoa, Ma! I'm stove up a bit, but I reckon I'll live. Right now I want to drag my aching carcass into the saddle and get back to the ranch where I can rest on something more comfortable than this washboard. Someone rustled our animals, though, so we'll have to double up."

"I'm afraid you're going to have to put up with this washboard for a few more hours." I knew from the look on her face that there was no point in arguing. "Bo has gone back to the ranch to fetch the buckboard and send for Doc O'Leary. Doc will meet us at the ranch as soon as he can, I'm sure.

Chad, Bill and Papa are trailing the horse thieves.
In the meantime, just rest. If you feel well enough
to talk, tell me what happened. If you don't, go
back to sleep. I can get the story from one of the
others."

Since just breathing hurt, I decided to let
Esther tell Ma what had happened. I reckoned
that even if I didn't sleep, I would at least be
spared the pain of talking. Before long, though, I
was asleep again.

My memories of the next four or five hours are
all mixed together like a stew. I had more night-
mares—the same ones. I drifted in and out of
sleep. I heard voices—mostly Ma's and Esther's,
but sometimes Tom's or Jasper's.

I ate again and drank more coffee and some
water. I remember lying there on my back for
what seemed like a long time. I wished Bo would
get back with the buckboard, yet I didn't want to
move again because of the pain. Those hours were
the most painful I'd ever known. I didn't know
how much longer I could stand the hurting.

When Bo showed up with the buckboard, things
went from bad to worse. He looked plenty worried
when he leaned over me and asked me how I felt.
I grinned and told him I was ready to hit the trail.
When he slid his strong arms under me, I gritted
my teeth and braced myself. My head was still
pounding. As Bo lifted me off that cot, I thought I
was tearing apart at the seams. Try as I did not to,
I screamed like a snake-bit heifer.

When he laid me in the back of the buckboard, I was still screaming. Bo kept saying how sorry he was. As he stepped back to let Ma see if she could make me more comfortable, I saw tears on his cheeks.

Ma did her best to pack me in the buckboard, and I reckon Bo had never driven as carefully as he did that day. Still, I felt as if I'd been roped, hogtied and dragged through the brush at a gallop, as we bounced toward the ranch. I wanted to show myself a man, but I cried and held Ma's hand most of the way home.

"Praise the Lord!" Ma said at last. "Doc O'Leary's buggy is tied up in front of the house."

"Whoa!" said Bo. The buckboard stopped.

My prayers had been answered. We had made the trip to the ranch, and I was still alive!

"What do you reckon would be the best way to...to...unload him, ma'am?" Bo asked, coming around to the back of the buckboard. "I can carry him into the—"

"No!" I moaned. "If that's your best idea, I have a better one."

"What is it, pard?"

"Put a coffin at the back of the buckboard," I said, grinning at Bo. "Slide me off so I drop right into it. Then nail the lid on and bury me. That will hurt less than having you carry me into the house."

Bo looked pretty sad until Ma started to laugh, then he laughed. I would have laughed too, had I not hurt so much.

Doc came out to the wagon, and he and Bo used the blankets under me as a stretcher to get me into the house. I won't say that the trip from the buckboard to the couch in the parlor was painless, but it was dead sure better than the trip from the shack to the buckboard had been.

Doc was one of the kindest people I knew. He was patient and gentle—and a good listener too. He and his wife must have been in their forties. She was his nurse when he needed one, and she was cut from the same bolt of cloth he had been as far as good qualities go. They almost always looked tired, but I had never heard either complain about anything.

I looked at Doc's pale face as he knelt beside the couch and said, smiling, "I need some information from you, son. Tell me briefly how you were injured and where you hurt. Then I'll examine you to see which limbs need to be amputated." He winked at me, and we both looked at Ma. She looked worried. "I'm only joshing, Mrs. Anderson," he said, trying to comfort her.

I told him about my dangling from the end of that lariat until that wall of water had hit me.

When I had finished, he smiled and shook his head slowly. "I declare, son, your guardian angel must have been hanging on that rope with you. Otherwise you'd be dead. I reckon you didn't have much time to take notice, but a flash flood like the one that cuffed you isn't just a big wave of water. Does this hurt?"

Doc began pressing gently on different places on my side as he talked. I let him know when he touched the sore places. "I've seen wild animals, cattle and horses, trees, wagons—even a stagecoach one time—swept along like wood chips in a creek."

He lifted my shirt and looked at my side. "Well, your skin isn't scratched or cut. Apparently the part of the flood that hit you was just water. Still, the force was great enough to crack at least three—maybe four—ribs."

Ma gasped. "Now don't you fret, Mrs. Anderson. Arty's young and strong, and boys like him mend quickly. He's going to have to spend at least a week in bed with these ribs wrapped tightly. Then for two or three weeks after he gets out of bed, he'll have to avoid strenuous activity."

He looked at me and continued: "That means keep off your horse for at least three weeks. By then the pain will let you know what you can or can't do. Be sure you listen to it. Before I go, I'm going to wrap those ribs. You're going to be pretty miserable for the next few days, but I'll leave a bottle of laudanum for the pain, and be back to check on you in a couple of days and to change the wrapping. Until then, your ma and grandma will take good care of you."

Later while Ma was walking Doc to the door, Grandma came in with a bottle of something and a spoon. "Are you ready for a dose of laudanum?" she asked.

"I'm ready for three doses."

She smiled. "Your mother says you've never had laudanum before. I'm sure one dose will be plenty."

I took the medicine, and Grandma was right: one dose was enough!

CHAPTER THIRTEEN

I woke up hungry—as usual. At least, my mind woke up. It seemed to be having trouble getting the rest of me to come along. I could hear Grandma asking me if I was ready to eat, but I couldn't see her. I smelled coffee and bacon, but I couldn't see them either. Somebody was sitting on my chest, digging me in the ribs with his spurs. When I realized what the problem was, I opened one eye.

"Well, hello, sleepyhead!" Grandma smiled at me as she set a tray of food on a chair. "Let's see if we can prop you up enough to strap on a feed bag."

Being a little woozy, I couldn't figure out why Grandma was bringing me supper in bed instead of letting me come to the table. When I raised up a mite to deal with whoever was riding my chest, I saw the wrapping and remembered everything. My head felt better, but I was having trouble herding all my thoughts into the same corral. Even with Grandma's help, the pain in my side from sitting up made me understand how a calf must feel when he gets branded.

"I'm sorry," Grandma said. "Did I hurt you?"

"No," I answered, trying to smile.

She propped me up with pillows and then set

the tray in my lap. I looked at the tray. Picking up
a fork, I said, "If you'd half killed me, Grandma,
to give me this kind of a supper, I'd have thanked
you anyway. *Gracias.*" She had brought me four
thick slices of bacon, three fried eggs, four biscuits,
a small bowl of sawmill gravy and a large mug
of coffee.

"This isn't your supper," she said, smiling.

"Whose is it?" I asked. "I hope you're not aiming
to take it away from me!"

"No," she said, laughing. "I'd be too afraid you'd
bite me if I tried to take your food. It's yours—it's
just not supper."

Daylight was coming through my window, but
not directly the way it did of an evening. "I reckon
I must have slept through supper," I said, pouring
gravy over two of the biscuits.

Grandma, still smiling, pulled the chair closer
to the side of my bed and sat down. "I reckon that's
not all you slept through."

I washed down a mouthful of bacon with a swig
of coffee, then ate a forkful of egg. I reckoned she'd
tell me what I wanted to know without my asking
a bunch of questions.

"That ain't your breakfast you're eating either;
it's your dinner," she added.

I almost choked on a bite of biscuit. I had slept
almost one whole day!

"Where is everybody?" I asked.

"Well, your mama's doing some of your chores.

And Grandpa's doing the rest of them."

"Grandpa's back?" I asked. "Did they catch the rustlers? Did they get Prince back?"

"Yes, yes and yes!" she replied.

"Well, what happened?"

"Keep eating," she said, "and I'll tell you. They rode in late yesterday afternoon with both the livestock and the rustler. He led them on a merry chase."

"There was only one man?" I asked.

"I didn't say anything about a man," Grandma answered.

"You said *he*," I replied. I crumbled the other two biscuits and poured the rest of the gravy over them. "That means the rustler had to be a man."

"Suppose you take a look at him and then make up your own mind," said Grandpa from the doorway.

"Howdy, Grandpa! Doc says I can't ride for two weeks—"

"Three weeks," interrupted Grandma, raising her eyebrows and looking at me over her spectacles.

"But I'll ride into town and look at him as soon as I can."

"I'm afraid he won't be there," Grandpa said, shaking his head.

"Why not?" I asked. "Where will he be?"

"Well, if I understand Chad and Bill correctly,

horse stealing is a hanging offense in this neck of the woods. Rather than go to the trouble of pestering the marshal and waiting for the circuit judge and having a trial—"

"Grandpa, you didn't...!" I swallowed the last bite of egg and hoped it would stay down. I felt dizzy for a few seconds, but Grandpa's answer settled me.

"String him up? We were fixing to; this one's a real hard case—won't say a word. Bill said we should let you see if you can get him to talk, although we did catch him red-handed."

"*Me* get him to talk? Has Bill gone loco?" I asked. I could feel my stomach beginning to knot. I was scared, angry—I stopped.

Grandpa was laughing. Reaching his left arm through the doorway behind him, he pulled an Indian boy into my room. He looked to be about a head shorter than me and two or three years younger. He was wearing a faded red calico shirt that looked big enough for two of him. The sleeves were rolled up to what should have been the elbow, but only his dark brown hands showed. In spite of the heat, he had buttoned the shirt right to the collar.

Looking at him, I reckoned that, as big as that shirt was and as small as he was, one unfastened button would have let that shirt fall down around his ankles.

He wore a dirty red bandana for a headband and a dirty gray one around his neck. Around his

small waist was a wide leather belt with an empty knife sheath on his right side. The shirt hung past his knees, but I could see that he wore high leather moccasins.

His dirty brown face had no expression on it. He held his head high and stared at me with his cold, black eyes.

Grandpa, standing behind the boy with one hand on each shoulder, smiled. "He hasn't spoken a single word since we caught him. Bill and I thought you might have better luck—not just yet, but in a few days when you're feeling better—if we can keep this young'un corralled that long."

"I...I don't know, Grandpa. I reckon he might be more likely to talk to me; but with me laid up, if he took a notion to light a shuck—"

"Oh, you'll have help," he said. "Two of your helpers are sorry-looking rascals, but I reckon the third one will make up for them."

Grandpa, keeping his hold on the boy, stepped to the side of the doorway. Tom, Jasper and Esther walked into the room, smiling.

"Grandpa, we'll get his story out of him. We have him outnumbered four to one. I reckon we'll have him talking in no time."

Now, four to one seemed to be plenty even if one of our four was Jasper. I had never had any dealing with an Apache before, but during the next few months, I often asked myself who outnumbered whom. Why, one time, that little horse thief stole my—oh, but that's a whole different story.

Esther and Jasper followed Grandpa and his prisoner out of the room, but Tom pulled a chair to the side of the bed. Smiling, he put on his hat, a brand-new black Stetson. "Pa says my old hat is probably somewhere in Mexico by now. I picked this one out myself. What do you think?"

"I think you look like a cowboy, pardner!" I replied. "Now we just need to round up a good horse and a saddle, and—"

"And I'd probably wind up killing it the way I did the first one," he said. Taking off his hat, he laid it in his lap and just sat there, looking at it for several minutes. Then he spoke quietly without looking up. "It's my fault that Prince and the other two animals got stolen too."

"Did you ride into that arroyo on purpose?" I asked.

Tom looked up surprised. "Arty! I—"

"I didn't think so," I said. "So how can any of what happened be your fault?"

He was looking at his hat again. "I'm a tinhorn. I...why are you laughing?"

"I think you mean greenhorn," I said, holding my side. "A tinhorn is a flashy gambler. A greenhorn is a new fellow like you who doesn't know his way around yet."

Without smiling, he answered, "All right, I'm a greenhorn. The thing is, if Esther, Jasper or you had been the last one out there, none of you would have ridden into that arroyo."

"Tom, from what I saw at the edge of that arroyo, your horse was as lost as you were. She got too close to the edge. The bank gave way, and she fell in. If any one of us had been riding her—or any other horse in the same place—the same thing would have happened. You can't blame yourself. Nobody else does."

Tom looked at me. "You're not just saying that to make me feel better?"

"Not likely," I replied, smiling. The chance I had been waiting for had come. I had noticed that when Grandpa had left, Esther had taken Jasper's hand and led him from the room. She had given me the chance to talk with Tom alone, and I was going to take it. She was probably somewhere in the house with Jasper, Ma, Grandpa, Grandma and any other believers who were around, praying that Tom would accept Christ.

"Tom," I asked, praying for wisdom, "did I ever tell you that I had been rescued once before—and from a worse mess than we were in the day before yesterday?"

"We almost died, Arty," replied Tom. He looked confused. "How much worse can a mess get?"

"I was born in an arroyo," I said. "This one was much deeper than the one where we were, and it didn't have a beginning or an end."

"I thought you were born back east—in Ohio," Tom said.

"Hear me out," I replied. "For the first six years of my life, I lived in that arroyo. I was happy because I didn't know there was more to life than where I was."

"Are you making this up?" Tom asked.

"No. One day I heard Ma calling from somewhere above me. When I looked up, I saw her standing way up on the rim of that arroyo. She was pointing at something behind me and yelling a warning."

"What was it?" Tom asked, his eyes wide as he leaned forward in his chair. He looked worried. "Are you getting too tired? I heard the doctor tell your ma to be sure you got plenty of rest."

My head was beginning to ache, but there was no way I was going to stop. "I'm fine," I answered. "Ma was pointing at another wall of water, roaring down that arroyo like a runaway locomotive."

"Bigger than the one that almost got us?" Tom asked, scooting his chair closer to my bed.

"Ten times—no, a hundred times bigger! I ran to the side where Ma was standing and tried to climb the bank."

"And you got out just in time?" Tom asked. Without realizing that he had done it, he grabbed the tin cup of water that Grandma had left on the washstand by my bed. He took a big swallow and put the cup back on the stand.

"No," I replied. "I did everything I could do to escape, but I couldn't get out on my own."

"So your ma pulled you out—just like our friends pulled us out, right?"

"Wrong!" I answered. "Ma tried. When I looked up, Pa had come to help. Grandma and Grandpa were there too, and so was Parson Sweeney. They all had ropes that were too short to reach me. They were all trying, but there was nothing they could do. Some were crying; some were praying." I drank the last swallow of my water.

"Are you going to tell me how you got out, or are you just teasing me?" Tom asked. His Stetson fell from his lap. Picking it up, he brushed it off and laid it on the bed.

"I've never been more serious in my life, pard. When I looked over my shoulder and saw that wall of water rushing at me, I knew I couldn't get out on my own. I knew that although my kinfolk and friends loved me, they couldn't save me either. I raised my hands toward Heaven—the same as I did the day before yesterday. A lariat dropped over my arms and tightened around my chest. I was pulled out of that arroyo that day to safe ground beside those who love me."

"Who saved you when nobody else could?" asked Tom. He was leaning so far forward that his arms were on my bed. He was gripping my bed sheet with both hands.

"His name is Jesus," I said quietly, "and He wants to save you too—"

"You *were* fooling me...no...lying to me with this story!" Tom grabbed his hat and stomped toward the door. He took a few steps and then turned around. "I don't know why you'd treat a 'pard' like this," he said. His red face had an angry look I'd never seen there before. "But I don't know if I care to be around you anymore!"

"No...wait, Tom," I began. He didn't really slam my bedroom door, but he made sure it was closed behind him.

I lay on my back and stared at the ceiling, not even trying to stop the tears. "Please bring him back, Father," I whispered. "Give me another chance."

CHAPTER FOURTEEN

The next two weeks were a time of learning and character building, and like most boys in similar situations, I was miserable much of the time. Tom did not come back to see me, and he avoided Jasper and Esther too. I prayed often for his salvation. Praying was one of the few things that Ma and Grandma would let me do.

During that first week I hadn't felt like doing anything else anyway. I was miserable because I was learning that no comfortable position exists for a fellow with broken ribs. I tried every possible position at least a dozen times, and none of them was comfortable.

I also learned that a person who plans to read should not take laudanum. I learned to let others help me to do what I had always thought to be simple tasks. A few times I had to let them do those tasks without any help from me.

The second week—especially toward the end of it—I started to feel a little better. At first I had prayed until I fell asleep. Once I had started to hurt a little less and had quit taking laudanum, I was wide awake much of the time. I read a book that Miss Ross had brought me. It was *Hard Times* by Charles Dickens, and she had told me

that reading it would make me appreciate our
school more. It wasn't my favorite book; in fact, I
would have had trouble reading it had I been able
to do anything else. Miss Ross had been right,
though: reading that book made me thankful for
our school and especially for her.

After I had finished praying and reading my
Bible each morning, Ma and Grandma would
bring me a grand breakfast. Usually whoever
brought my food would visit with me while I ate.
In this way I kept up with what was happening on
the ranch and in town while I was locked in my
cell. Almost every day I listened with delight to
news of the horse thief's latest attempt to escape
from the ranch.

"He refuses to speak," Grandma told me the day
after our ranch "posse" had captured him. "He
won't even tell us his name, so we've named him
'Apache Boy' for now. He hates your grandfather
and me, I reckon," she said, smiling.

"Why?" I asked.

"I'm afraid we insulted him," she replied.

"How?" I asked. She really had my attention. I
couldn't picture my grandparents insulting anyone.

"He was filthy, so we heated water, filled the tub
and made him understand that he needed to take
a bath."

"And he took offense because you asked him to
take a bath?" I asked.

"Not exactly," she replied. "He refused to bathe."

I reckoned this story was going to be a good one. Grandma had those same red splotches on her neck that Ma gets sometimes. "What did you and Grandpa do?" I asked. I was pretty sure I knew the answer, but I couldn't wait to hear her tell it.

"Your grandfather and Bo bathed him," she said quietly.

"Both of them bathed him?" I asked, trying not to grin.

"It was a two-person job," she replied. "One held that little wildcat while the other scrubbed."

"Did they get him bathed?" I asked, trying hard not to laugh at the picture in my head.

"Of course they did." She stood and straightened her dress. "Did I say something amusing?" she asked, looking at me over the top of her spectacles.

"No, ma'am," I replied, biting my lower lip to keep from laughing, "but I reckon you could."

She snatched my tray, turned and walked to the door. For a few seconds she stood in the open doorway with her back to me. When she turned to face me, she was laughing. "If you must know," she said, "by the time they had finished, all three of them had taken baths!" She turned, still laughing, and left the room.

Marshal Bodie stopped by one day, and we played a game of chess. Esther came over two or three times—once with some cookies she had baked. Jasper came two or three times each week. Sometimes during the first week I didn't even know he was there. Ma said he had just sat in a chair by my bed, sometimes talking to me quietly, sometimes praying, sometimes crying.

From time to time each of the hands stopped by for a few minutes. Their visits had to be brief because—as they enjoyed reminding me—someone had to work the ranch while I was just lying around.

As enjoyable as all of those visits were, they left a lot of empty hours in the days after I started to feel better. I have always had a good imagination, but I learned the meaning of boredom during those long days of recovery.

One afternoon early in the third week of my jail term, I was sitting in my bed reading *The Prairie* by James Fenimore Cooper. Ma had propped me up with what I reckoned must have been every pillow in the house. The part of the story I was reading right then, though, had me sitting up straight and paying close attention. I didn't hear the door to my room open.

"Can I talk to you?" Tom asked.

I didn't scream like a little girl, but I came mighty close. I did drop the book.

"I'm sorry, Arty," said Tom, taking a step backwards. "I didn't mean to scare you."

Being a boy, I wanted to say that he hadn't scared me at all. When someone scares you just a little, you can get away with saying that. Tom had scared me more than just a little, and he knew it. I grinned and picked up the book. "It's all right.

You caught me at a good part of the story. Pull up a chair."

Tom hung his hat on one of the bedposts at the foot of my bed, pulled a chair over next to me and sat down. Leaning forward with his elbows on his knees, he looked at the floor and tapped the ends of his fingers together. Two or three minutes passed.

"Take your time, pard," I said.

Tom looked at me, then asked, "Am I still your pard?"

"I don't recollect having heard different," I said. "Have you?"

"No," he replied, smiling. "No, I haven't."

"Then I reckon you can start talking."

Tom ran the fingers of both hands through his hair and took a deep breath. "I was pretty hot when I left here last time."

"I thought so," I said smiling.

He gave a kind of half smile and said, "I really thought you had just told me one of your tales. I was feeling pretty stupid for believing you."

"I was telling you the truth. I reckon I buttered it up a bit to make it easier for you to swallow."

"I understand that now," he said. "My parents have been worried about me since I came home that day. I thought they'd never let me out of their sight again after what happened to us on our ride. Instead, they told me that they knew they needed to start letting me be out with my friends. They said that when I came home safe, they realized they had been wrong in keeping me cooped up because of Dan's accident."

"That's great news!"

"I know," he replied, "but I didn't think so at the time. I told them I didn't have any friends and that I wanted to stay home. They were surprised, and they wanted to know what had happened."

"Did you tell them?" I asked.

"Not until last night. I just didn't want to talk about it. My mother had kept asking me every day or two if I wanted to talk. Last night when she came to my room to say good night, she asked again. I was ready."

"What did you tell her?"

"I told her your whole story—just like you told it to me," he said.

"What did she say?"

Tom looked at the floor and began tapping his fingers again. After a long pause he looked up at me with tears in his eyes. "She cried, Arty. The only other time I've seen her cry like that was when Dan died. When she finally stopped, she explained to me what you were trying to tell me. She said she understood because God had done the same thing for her when she was just a little girl."

"That's great!" I said.

"She said she and my grandparents were God-fearing people who went to church regularly."

"What went wrong?" I asked.

"That was my question too," Tom answered. "My

father has never had any interest in God or church. When he started courting my mother, my grandparents warned her to stay away from him. She wouldn't listen because she was sure she could change him after they got married."

"But she couldn't," I said.

"No," he replied. "She said my father was never unkind when she tried to get him to take her to church. He just wasn't interested. She stopped going to church just before Dan was born. She never went back."

"That's a sad story," I said.

"I'm not done yet," he said, wiping his eyes on the back of his sleeve. "I came here to give you some good news. My mother told me that one summer when Dan was visiting our grandparents, Grandpa told him about Jesus. Dan asked Jesus to come into his heart. When Dan died, he went to Heaven."

"Yes, he did," I said. "Wouldn't you like to invite Jesus into your heart too? Then someday you'll see Dan again and be with him forever."

"I can't," Tom sighed, looking at the floor and tapping his fingers together again. He began to squirm around like he was sitting on a hot stove.

"Why not, Tom?" I asked.

He jumped out of his chair with a big grin on his face. "Because I already did last night! And Mother and I are coming to church Sunday, and we're going to try to get my father to come too! Will you and your family pray for him?"

With tears in my eyes and a lump in my throat, I prayed with Tom right then.

That next Sunday I was set free long enough to go to church. Singing made my ribs hurt, but I couldn't help myself. I was sitting one bench behind Tom, who was sitting between his mother *and* father. I could only see the back of Tom's head, but I knew he was smiling. So was I.

For a complete list of books available from the Swordʼof the Lord, write to Sword of the Lord Publishers, P. O. Box 1099, Murfreesboro, Tennessee 37133.

(800) 251-4100
(615) 893-6700
FAX (615) 848-6943
www.swordofthelord.com